THE DOLL HOSPITAL

FOR MOM, FOR ALL HER SEWING
WHEN I WAS YOUNG
–K. G.

FOR MOM, WHO TAKES CARE OF EVERYONE
–S. G.

ATHENEUM BOOKS FOR YOUNG READERS • An imprint of Simon & Schuster Children's Publishing Division • 1230 Avenue of the Americas, New York, New York 10020 • Text copyright © 2018 by Kallie George • Illustrations copyright © 2018 by Sara Gillingham • All rights reserved, including the right of reproduction in whole or in part in any form. • ATHENEUM BOOKS FOR YOUNG READERS is a registered trademark of Simon & Schuster, Inc. Atheneum logo is a trademark of Simon & Schuster, Inc. • For information about special discounts for bulk purchases, please contact Simon & Schuster Special Sales at 1-866-506-1949 or business@simonandschuster.com. • The Simon & Schuster Speakers Bureau can bring authors to your live event. For more information or to book an event, contact the Simon & Schuster Speakers Bureau at 1-866-248-3049 or visit our website at www.simonspeakers.com. • Jacket design by Sara Gillingham and Sonia Chaghatzbanian; interior design by Sonia Chaghatzbanian • The text for this book was set in Futura. • The illustrations for this book were created with cut paper, fabric, stuffing, a computer, and ink. • Manufactured in China • 0318 SCP • First Edition • 10 9 8 7 6 5 4 3 2 1 • Library of Congress Cataloging-in-Publication Data • Names: George, Kallie, author. | Gillingham, Sara, illustrator. • Title: The doll hospital / by Kallie George ; illustrated by Sara Gillingham. • Description: First edition. | New York : Atheneum Books for Young Readers, [2018] | Summary: Dr. Pegs and the Nesting Nurses have a very busy day repairing dolls—and even Teddy—at the Doll Hospital. • Identifiers: LCCN 2016058372 | ISBN 9781534401211 (hardcover) | ISBN 9781534401228 (eBook) • Subjects: | CYAC: Dolls—Repairing—Fiction. • Classification: LCC PZ7.G293326 Dol 2018 | DDC [E]—dc23 • LC record available at https://lccn.loc.gov/2016058372

THE DOLL HOSPITAL

BY KALLIE GEORGE AND SARA GILLINGHAM

 ATHENEUM BOOKS FOR YOUNG READERS

atheneum New York London Toronto Sydney New Delhi

The sun rises like a golden button in the sky.

Dr. Pegs is enjoying a calm morning at the Doll Hospital.

Nobody is sick.
Everything is organized.
There is only one thing
on her checklist:

• sort the buttons

"Easy-peasy," says Pegs.
"I can do it right now."

She is about to start when . . .

DING-A-LING-A-LING!

The emergency bells ring.

It's Portia, a porcelain doll.

Uh-oh! Portia's arm is cracked.
"It's okay," says Pegs.
"A bit of glue is all you need."

Pegs adds to her list:

- glue Portia's arm
- sort the buttons

Pegs is about to get the glue when . . .

DING-A-LING-A-LING!

The emergency bells ring.

It's Scoop, a stuffed doll.
He has a stomachache.

"It's okay," says Pegs.
"You just need some new stuffing."

Pegs adds to her list:

- stuff Scoop's stomach
- glue Portia's arm
- sort the buttons

Pegs is about to get the stuffing when . . .

DING-A-LING-A-LING!

The emergency bells ring.

It's Baby, a talking doll.
Her pull string is all knotted up.

Instead of saying "Mommy," she says,

"MOO!"

"Oh, that won't do," says Pegs.
"We must fix your voice."

Pegs adds to her list:

- untangle Baby's string

- stuff Scoop's stomach

• glue Portia's arm

• sort the buttons

The list is growing.
And Pegs hasn't checked anything off yet!

DING-A-LING-A-LING!

ANOTHER patient! Oh no!

Teddy? But this is a *doll* hospital!

Of course Dr. Pegs will take care of him.
But her list is *so* long! "Help!" she cries.

She rings a special bell.

DONG-

DONG-

DONG!

Help arrives!
It's the Nesting Nurses.

ONE,

TWO,

THREE,

FOUR,

AND
FIVE!

They push two beds together
for Teddy and settle him in.
Then Pegs and the Nesting Nurses
get to work.

They untangle
Baby's string.

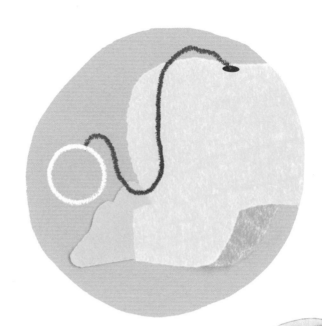

They stuff
Scoop's stomach.

They glue
Portia's arm.

They even find the
perfect button for Teddy's eye—
after they sort the buttons.

At last, everyone is feeling better.

"Time to sleep,"
says Pegs.
"You will get to
go home tomorrow."

Once everyone is tucked in,

Pegs turns to the Nesting Nurses.

"I couldn't have done it without you. Thank you," she says.

Now it's time for Pegs to get some rest too.

The moon shines like
silver thread in the sky.

Another day is done
at the Doll Hospital.